Awake in the Dark!

Story by Dawn McMillan
Illustrations by Roberto Fino

Contents

Chapter 1
Driving the Go-karts

Cody and Theo were on their way to a holiday camp in the country. As Cody's dad drove along the dusty road, the boys talked excitedly about the things that they could do at camp.

"I want to go kayaking!" exclaimed Theo.

"I've always wanted to drive a go-kart," grinned Cody.

Dad drove the car up a drive, and parked it alongside a big building.

"This must be the camp kitchen and dining room," said Cody, as the boys climbed out of the car.

"And that other building must be where they have games and concerts," added Theo.

"You're just in time for lunch," called the camp leader, who had come over to meet them. "But first I'll take you to your cabin. You're all in Cabin 5, and this afternoon it's your turn for the go-karts."

"The go-karts!" shouted Cody. "Quick, Theo. Let's get our things organised, and have lunch!"

After lunch, Theo, Cody and Dad put on their safety helmets and walked to the go-kart track.

"I hope my leg will fit in the kart," said Cody, looking worried.

"It will," said Theo reassuringly, "and you'll be able to use your other leg for the pedals. Come on, let's have a practice drive."

"Now, not too fast to begin with," said the instructor. "Get the feel of the steering, and the brakes."

"Great!" shouted Theo, as he and Cody came out of the first corner.

"Oh, no!" shouted Dad, as he spun his kart right off the track.

Chapter 2

There's Someone Out There

That night, as they climbed into their sleeping bags, the boys were still laughing about Dad's go-kart driving.

"I hope I do better with the climbing wall tomorrow," Dad said. "Now, lights out!"

Soon the cabin was quiet. Theo lay awake in the dark, thinking about the climbing wall.

"Cody!" he whispered, "I'm worried about climbing the wall tomorrow. I might fall!"

"You won't fall, Theo," replied Cody, "and, anyway, they'll have safety equipment. I'm worried about tomorrow night's concert. We have to make up a play about camp, and no-one in here knows what to do!"

"We'll think of something," said Theo, as he pulled his sleeping bag over his shoulders. "And I will climb the wall!"

Theo was almost asleep when he heard a noise. He held his breath. There it was again. . . footsteps, and a snuffling sound!

He sat up and looked around the cabin. Everyone was asleep. The noise was coming from outside.

Quickly, Theo climbed down to where Cody was sleeping in the bottom bunk.

"Cody! Wake up!" he whispered. "There's someone walking around outside the cabin!"

Cody sat up, wide awake. "I can't hear anything!" he whispered.

"Listen!" Theo whispered back. "Can you hear it now?"

"Yes, I can!" replied Cody anxiously. "And what's that creaking noise?"

"Someone's trying to open the door!" said Theo.

"It's not the door," Cody whispered. "It's coming from that corner. Let's take a look from the window."

Chapter 3

There It Is Again!

The boys peered out of the window, into the moonlight. Close to the cabin, there was the outline of a fence. A little further away, large trees cast a shadow across the field.

"I can't see anything," said Theo.

"Shh!" whispered Cody. "There it is again!"

"Open the door, Theo," whispered Cody.

"Do you think I should?" asked Theo nervously.

"Well, just open it a little bit," replied Cody. "It could be the wind in the trees."

Quietly, Theo opened the cabin door. "It's not the wind!" he gasped. "The wind doesn't snuffle and creak like that! Let's get your dad!"

"Boys!" whispered a voice behind them. "What are you doing?"

Cody and Theo turned to see Dad's shape in the dark.

"Shh!" said Cody. "Dad! Listen! There's something out there! Theo heard a noise, and when I woke up I heard it, too."

"You were dreaming. . ." Dad began to explain.

"Dad!" interrupted Cody. "It wasn't a dream! Listen!"

"You're right!" Dad answered. "There is something there! Wait here, boys. I've got my torch. I'll see what it is."

Chapter 4

In the Torchlight

Theo and Cody waited in the cabin.

"I hope Dad's all right!" whispered Cody.

Suddenly, Cody heard his dad call softly, "Open the door, boys."

"What is it, Dad?" Cody asked.

"Come out here and see," said Dad, "but stay behind me where you'll be safe."

As Theo pushed the door open, Cody thought he heard his father laugh.

"It's so dark!" whispered Cody, as he and Theo followed behind Dad.

"We can't see anything!" said Theo, trying to sound brave.

When Dad reached the corner of the cabin, he whispered, "Boys, I'd like you to meet. . . Daisy!"

A large black cow blinked her eyes in the torchlight as she rubbed her head against the fence.

"It's a cow!" laughed Cody. "Theo, we were scared of a cow!"

"She's snuffling as she breathes, and it's the fence that's creaking!" laughed Theo.

"Hey, Cody," Theo laughed again, "we can make up a play about Daisy for the concert. You and I will be Daisy, underneath my black sleeping bag!"

"You could do your play in the dark," suggested Dad, "and then I could turn on the torch!"

"Good idea, Dad!" laughed Cody.